JULIE SYKES

ILLUSTRATED BY

THAN REED

D1426229

For Daniel and Jamie – J.S.
For Joseph – N.R.

First published 2009 by Macmillan Children's Books
a division of Macmillan Publishers Limited
20 New Wharf Road, London N1 9RR
Basingstoke and Oxford
Associated companies throughout the world
www.panmacmillan.com

ISBN 978-0-330-51045-5

1 3 5 7 9 8 6 4 2

A CIP catalogue record for this book is available from the British Library.

Printed and bound in the UK by CPI Mackays, Chatham, ME5 8TD

CONTENTS

CHAPTER ONE
SEAGULL TOWERS

The phone was ringing. Max dashed out of his bedroom, raced down the stairs and snatched it up.

'Hello,' he said. 'This is Max the Pet Sitter.'

'Hello, Max,' said a cheery voice. 'This is Ned Nettles the Pet Owner. Can you pet-sit for me? I'm going away for a week to help my sister out. She runs a youth club and one of her staff is sick.'

'Sure,' said Max. 'What sort of pet have you got?'

'A puppy,' said Ned. 'He's adorable.

Why not come over and meet him? I live at Flat 6, Seagull Towers.'

'I'm on my way,' said Max, and put the phone down.

Max wrote Ned's address in his pet sitter's notebook, then hurried out to the garden to get his bike from the shed. Mum was weeding the rose bed.

'Going somewhere?' she asked, waving the trowel at him.

'Seagull Towers, to meet a puppy and a man called Ned Nettles.'

'That'll be fun,' said Mum. 'You've always wanted a puppy.'

It was true. Max desperately wanted a pet of his own, but he couldn't have one because his annoying big sister, Alice, was allergic to animals. As Max cycled to Seagull Towers he wondered what the puppy would be like. Ned Nettles had called his pet adorable, and Max imagined a cute little animal with floppy ears and big brown eyes. Ned sounded nice too. Max decided he would be young and friendly with a smiley face.

It wasn't far to Seagull Towers. Max pedalled up the drive and stopped in surprise by a large sign.

'Seagull Towers,' he read. 'No Skate-boards. No Ball Games. No Pets. By Order of the Caretaker.'

That couldn't be right! Max pulled his pet sitter's notebook out of his pocket to check he had the right address.

He was flicking through the pages when a voice called out, 'Hello, are you Max?'

Max looked up. Seagull Towers was a huge old house with three floors and two turrets. A very grand stone staircase led up to an enormous revolving front door, and standing at the top of it was a wrinkled old man with spiky silver hair.

'Max?' he called again, and when Max nodded the man swung a leg over the stone handrail and slid down the banister.

'Ned Nettles,' he said, landing almost on Max's toes. 'Thanks for coming so quickly.'

SEAGULL TOWERS
No Skateboa
No Ball Gam
No Pets
BY ORDER of th

'All part of the service,' said Max, trying not to laugh.

Since taking his first pet-sitting job Max had met all sorts of unusual pets and their owners, and Ned was no exception! There was green glitter in his spiky silver hair and he wore star-shaped green and silver glasses. Pinned to his black shirt was a life-like spider badge. He wasn't a bit like Max had imagined.

'Park your bike there. Then you can meet Fang,' said Ned.

Max pointed at the sign. 'But I thought . . .'

'Thinking can be dangerous,' Ned interrupted. 'Hurry up.'

As Max chained his bike to the signpost something hit him in the back of the legs.

'Oomph!' he spluttered, almost head-butting his back wheel. He spun round.

'Woo, woo, wooooo!' panted an untidy bundle of grey fur. 'Woo, woo, wooooo!'

'Nice dog,' said Max, hesitantly putting out a hand, then pulling it back again when he saw the size of Fang's teeth.

7

'Quiet, Fang,' hissed Ned, and then, 'Fang, that's naughty.'

Fang was attacking the signpost. Ned pulled him away, then prized a long splinter of wood from the puppy's mouth.

'How many times have I told you not to chew?' he said, pretending to be cross.

Max gasped. Fang's teeth must be really sharp to do that amount of damage. He hoped the puppy was going to be friendly. It would be awful if Fang decided to take a chunk out of him!

'Fang, say hello to Max.'

Ned let the puppy go again.

'Woooooo, woo, woo, wooooo!' squealed Fang, rushing back to Max.

Fang had wolf-like blue eyes, a long snout and wicked claws. Max tensed as Fang jumped towards him, but the puppy

only wanted to lick him.
Max laughed, patting
the bits of the leaping
Fang he could reach,
until he realized he
was standing in a
puddle.

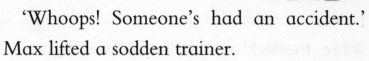

'Whoops! Someone's had an accident.'
Max lifted a sodden trainer.

'That's no accident.' Ned grinned. 'It's a
compliment. Fang's excited. He only does
that when he really likes someone.'

'Nice!' said Max. 'So what does he do to
people he doesn't like?'

Ned tapped the side of his nose.
'Best not ask,' he said.

CHAPTER TWO
A SECRET

'**C**ome and see my flat,' said Ned once Fang had calmed down.

He hurried up the stone staircase and Max had to run to catch him as he disappeared through the revolving door. Max followed, and the door whisked him round and spat him out so quickly that he landed on his bottom in the reception hall. A large woman with a chin as bristly as a porcupine peered over the counter.

'Morning, Ned, and who's that?'

Ned hauled Max to his feet.

'This is Max the Plant Sitter. He's going

to water my plants for me while I'm away.
Max, meet Bertha Crab, our caretaker.'

Max opened his mouth to correct Ned,
then shut it again in surprise as Ned slyly
kicked his ankle. He looked around for
Fang, but the puppy seemed to have
disappeared.

'Hello, Bertha,' said Max.

'It's Mrs Crab to you,' sniffed the

caretaker, glaring at Max. 'I hope you're going to behave yourself. The rules are clearly—'

'Yes, yes,' interrupted Ned impatiently. 'Thank you, Bertha, but we've got to dash. Come along, Max.'

Ned's flat was in one of the turrets. He led the way up a spiral staircase to a corridor on the first floor and stopped at a door numbered six.

'Here we are.'

Deftly Ned unpinned his spider badge and threw it at the door. A long silver thread, attached to a tiny cobweb on Ned's shirt, followed the spider. When it hit the door the spider scuttled up to the lock, stuck one leg inside the keyhole and wiggled it. The door opened.

Max gawped, then jumped as Fang suddenly appeared by his feet.

'Where did you get to?' he asked as the puppy barged past him.

'Fang is very good at being invisible,' chuckled Ned. He popped the spider back on his shirt. 'In you go, Max.'

Max stepped inside Ned's flat, curiously peeping into the rooms as Ned led the way to the kitchen. In the lounge stars dangled from the ceiling, and in the bedroom there was everything from a cauldron to a pointed green hat.

'Why did you tell Mrs Crab I'm a Plant Sitter?' he asked.

'Haven't you worked it out yet?' Ned stopped and shook his head. 'And I thought you were clever!'

'You said that thinking can be dangerous,' Max reminded him.

Ned roared with laughter. 'True, but I need some excitement, living here. There are far too many silly rules. No skateboards, no ball games, NO PETS. No fun, if you ask me.'

'Sounds about as interesting as watching a cauldron rust,' Max agreed.

'It was!' said Ned. 'Until I found Fang. Someone left him on the beach, tied up in a sack, with the tide coming in. How could they! Fang's the most adorable werepup in the world.'

'A werepup?!' exclaimed Max. 'Wicked.'

'Wicked he is too,' Ned agreed. 'Spider's teeth, Fang has livened things up! I've had to keep Fang a secret because of the silly no-pets rule, but I've had him for over a week and no one's guessed yet! Not even nosey old Bertha Crab.'

'So, if anyone asks, I'm here to look after your plants.'

'That's right,' said Ned, perching against the kitchen table. 'You mustn't tell anyone about Fang.'

'How do I take him out for walks?' asked Max.

Ned opened a cupboard and brought out an enormous wicker basket with a frilly red cover.

'You have to smuggle

him out of the building in this,' he announced.

Max eyed the basket suspiciously.

'No way! I'll look like Little Red Riding Hood!' he protested.

Ned's cheerful face turned serious.

'Bertha Crab, the caretaker, is even crabbier than her name suggests. If she finds out about Fang, then she'll make him leave, or worse. Bertha used to have a dog, until it chewed her favourite slippers. She was so mad she said the dog was dangerous and made the vet put it to sleep.'

'That's evil!' exclaimed Max.

'I know.' Ned gripped Max's arm. 'That's why you have to promise to keep Fang a secret.'

'I promise,' said Max solemnly. 'I'm good at secrets. I get tons of practice with my sister, Alice. She's got more nose than an aardvark.'

'Good,' said Ned. 'You'll have to be very careful. Bertha Crab is a pain. She's never around when you need her, yet she's sure to turn up like a nasty rash when you don't. And there's one more thing: remember, Fang is a werepup. Never take him out at night. NEVER! There's a full moon soon and anything could happen! Got that? Right, I'll show you what he eats. You'll also need a key and your wages.'

Chapter Three
Howling in the Night

Max couldn't wait to start pet-sitting Fang. He loved animals, and he loved a challenge, but the first challenge came quicker than he thought. When Max arrived at Seagull Towers the following morning Mrs Crab was waiting for him.

'There was an awful racket last night,' she said, glaring at him over the counter in the reception hall. 'It was coming from Ned's flat and it sounded like an animal.'

Max's stomach turned a somersault. The noise had to be Fang, but why? Max hoped he wasn't hurt.

Mrs Crab stood up.

'I think I'd better come with you and investigate.'

Max did some quick thinking.

'Sorry, Mrs Crab,' he apologized. 'Ned must have left the stereo on. He loves listening to music.'

'Music!' exclaimed Mrs Crab. 'That was music? It sounded like an animal in pain.'

'It was probably opera.' Max fumbled in his pocket for Ned's spare key. 'That's painful to listen to.'

Quickly Max climbed the spiral staircase, then hurried along the corridor. It was very quiet. Too quiet. Max felt slightly sick and wasn't sure whether it was due to the winding staircase or worry. Something fluttered in his hand as he pulled out the spare spider badge Ned had given him. He opened his palm, jumping as the spider leaped for the door.

'What was that?'

Max spun round. Mrs Crab had followed him upstairs.

'Nothing,' he said, raising his hand to the door and pretending to unlock it, even though the spider was doing the job quite nicely by itself.

'Bye, Mrs Crab.'

Max slid round the door, then shut it

again quickly. There was a squeak and a loud thud from the other side. Max lifted the letter box and saw the caretaker squashed against the flat door like a bug on a car windscreen. Silently chuckling to himself, he

headed for the kitchen to see what had upset Fang.

Max pushed open the kitchen door and gasped at the mess inside. The table lay upside down in the corner of the room. Two chairs were on the cooker. The dustbin was wedged inside the washing machine and a mountain of food covered the floor; perched seesaw-like on the food mountain was a broken shelf.

'Fang,' called Max. 'Fang, where are you?'

'Help!'

Max spun round. He'd expected Fang to

bark, not talk. Was someone playing a joke?

'Fang, is that you?'

'Well, it's not Ned,' replied Fang smartly.

Max grinned. He'd looked after talking animals before, but it was still a surprise to hear an animal speak for the first time. Max picked his way through the mess until he saw a black nose peeping out from beneath a box of Witchos.

'What happened?' he asked, pulling the Witchos aside. 'Were you hungry?'

'Starving,' agreed Fang, wriggling free.

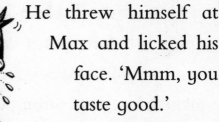

He threw himself at Max and licked his face. 'Mmm, you taste good.'

'Yuk!' Max pushed the puppy away. 'Go and lick something else.'

Fang stopped licking Max's face and started on his shoes.

'What happened here then?' asked Max.

'I don't know,' said Fang sheepishly. 'It was almost a full moon last night. I could see it through a chink in the curtain and it made me want to howl. Then I got hungry and went to get a snack. Only my biscuits are on the top shelf and I couldn't reach them. I was nibbling one of Ned's sticks to take my mind off my rumbly tummy when suddenly there was a bang and everything fell on top of me. I howled for help, but no one came.'

'No one knows you're here,' said Max. 'Ned's keeping you a secret because of the no-pets rule. No more howling. If you get found out, you'll have to leave.'

Fang's blue eyes grew as large as cauldrons.

'I don't want to leave. Ned's soooo nice!'

Max bent to pick up the chewed stick.

'Are you sure you're allowed to have this?'

'Yes,' said Fang, licking Max's nose. 'It's not Ned's best one. It's a spare. Mmmm, you taste scrummy.'

'Get off!' laughed Max.

The stick looked familiar, but it was so

25

badly chewed that Max couldn't work out its function so he propped it against the washing machine.

'I'll clear up while you're eating breakfast. Then we'll go out.'

'Yippee!' squealed Fang.

Max slid his rucksack from his back and dropped it on the floor.

'I brought sandwiches, drinks and a ball. I thought we could go to the beach. I know a nice one that's never busy.'

'Ooooh! Yes, yes, yes!' Fang ran round in excited circles, almost knocking Max over.

'Calm down!' laughed Max.

Ned had left a huge supply of puppy food. Max dished up a whole can of Meaty Chunks, mixed it with a handful of dog biscuits, then refilled Fang's water bowl with fresh water. He tidied up the kitchen while Fang ate.

'I'll put the broken shelf here,' he said, laying it on a worktop. 'Please don't break anything else. Ned won't be happy if he comes back to a wrecked flat.'

Fang grunted. He was busy pushing his bowl around in circles on the floor as he licked it clean.

'Yummy,' he sighed. 'That was delicious.'

The wicker basket to smuggle Fang from the building was next to a blackened cauldron. Under the silly frilly lid Max found a collar, an extending lead, a small plastic shovel for scooping up poo and a stack of plastic bags to put the poo in.

'Nice,' he said, pushing it up one end to make room. 'In you get.'

The moment Fang dived into the basket there was a loud crack. 'Whoops!' yelped Fang. 'Didn't see that there.'

'Fatty!' Max laughed, picking up the broken shovel. 'Luckily for me, it's the handle end that broke.'

Max pulled the cover back over the basket and pushed the stray tufts of Fang's grey fur out of sight.

'Ready?' he asked.

'Ready,' was the muffled reply.

'Don't make a sound. I don't even want to hear you breathing,' Max joked.

Chapter Four
Where is Mrs Crab?

Max needed both hands to lift the basket. He staggered a few paces, then dumped it on the floor.

'Oomph!' he groaned. 'What a weight!'

'Must be those Meaty Chunks,' said Fang.

'It's this meaty chunk,' teased Max, pulling back the cover and poking Fang's round tummy. 'You're too heavy for me to carry you in this. How does Ned manage?'

'Ned doesn't use the basket. He says a funny rhyme that makes me invisible,' said Fang.

'Cool!' said Max. He'd guessed Ned was a wizard from some of the things he kept in his flat. That must be how he had got Fang out and then back inside the flats yesterday when they'd first met. He'd said the puppy was good at being invisible. Max realized that Ned hadn't been joking.

'Well, I can't do magic so I'll have to find another way of sneaking you outside.'

Max thought for a moment and then had a brainwave.

'You can ride in my rucksack. It's much lighter than the basket.'

It was a squeeze to fit Fang in the rucksack. Max left the zip partly open so he could breathe.

'Wheeee! This is FUN!' shouted Fang, as Max hoisted the bag on to his back.

'Shh!' whispered Max. 'We're leaving now.'

Max opened the door to the flat and cautiously headed for the stairs. He wished he'd remembered to tell Fang to keep still. Every now and then the puppy wriggled, which was a bit of a giveaway. But he needn't have worried. There was no sign of Mrs Crab in the reception hall, but there was a long line of people at the counter waiting to see her.

'She's never around when she's needed,' grumbled one.

'I spend half my days looking for her,' added another.

Nervously Max looked around. Where

had Mrs Crab gone after she'd followed him up to Ned's flat? Maybe she was hiding somewhere, waiting to catch him out? She had to be up to something, or she would be back in reception by now doing her job. Well, she wasn't going to catch Max out. He was a good pet sitter. No way was he going to let Mrs Crab find out about Fang. Ned had made it very clear what Mrs Crab would do to Fang if she caught him. She'd make him leave, or worse.

'Mrs Crab is evil,' Max muttered as he hurried to the door.

Safely outside, Max stood at the bottom of the stone steps while he decided on the quickest way to the beach.

'Pssst,' whispered Fang. 'You can let me out now.'

Max waited until he was almost at the

end of the drive before he stopped. The rucksack was heavy and he was glad to wriggle out of it and let Fang free. The moment Max unzipped his rucksack Fang leaped out and stretched his legs.

Suddenly a grey squirrel burst out from a bush.

'Yummy! A squirrel,' shouted Fang, tearing after it.

'Fang!' cried Max as the two animals raced back towards the flats.

Max chased after Fang, calling, 'Come back before someone sees you.'

Fang ignored him and chased the squirrel

into the back garden. Petals fell like confetti as the werepup hurtled through a large bed of autumn flowers. Max sprinted closer and dived for the puppy, but Fang wriggled free and Max was left clutching a tuft of grey fur.

Ned was right about Fang being a handful, thought Max.

Fang wasn't going to stay a secret for long if he carried on like this.

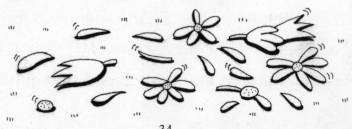

CHAPTER FIVE
ROCKET PAWS

Eventually Max caught up with the puppy at the base of a tree.

'Squirrel – one, Fang – zero, and serves you right,' he said, crossly.

'I only wanted to lick it,' said Fang forlornly. 'Squirrels taste yummy.'

Max pulled Fang's lead out of his rucksack and buckled the collar around his neck.

'Urrrrrrrrggh!' yelled Fang. 'That's strangling me.'

Max slid a finger through the collar to check that it wasn't secured too tightly.

'It isn't!'

'It is!' said Fang crossly.

'Ned said I had to keep you a secret. Some secret! What if Mrs Crab had seen you?'

Fang hung his head. 'I'm sorry.'

'That's OK.'

'Will you take this off me now?'

'No way!'

'Not moving then,' said Fang, plonking his fat bottom down on the ground.

'Suit yourself,' said Max. 'We won't go to the beach.'

Max chuckled as Fang immediately leaped up, barking, 'Come on, slow toes.'

'Not so fast, rocket paws,' said Max, holding Fang back as he rushed towards the gate at the end of the garden.

The gate led to a bushy lane. At first Fang walked nicely by Max's side, but the werepup was too excited to stay there for long. Soon he was darting ahead or lagging behind to sniff at interesting smells. Each time Fang pulled in a different direction the extending lead got longer.

'It's like having a dog on a yo-yo,' Max laughed.

Luckily the beach wasn't far. The moment Fang's paws stepped on to the sand the werepup yelped with delight.

'Wait!'

Max almost had his arm pulled off as Fang galloped towards the farthest end of the beach before he stopped.

'That was great, wasn't it?' he panted.

'Yeah, great! If you like being tied to the end of a rocket,' agreed Max, spitting sand from his mouth.

He sat down and Fang jumped in his lap

to lick his face.

'Pooh! Get off! Your breath pongs!'

'So does yours,' said Fang cheerfully.

Max unclipped Fang's lead. He rummaged in his rucksack for a ball and threw it across the beach.

'Fang, fetch.'

'Fetch it yourself. You threw it,' said Fang.

Max looked at him suspiciously.

'It's a game. I throw a ball. You go and fetch it.'

'I'll do the throwing then,' said Fang.

'That's not how the game's played.'

'Then it's a stupid game,' said Fang. 'Let's dig a hole instead. We can both do that.'

Enthusiastically Fang began to dig, spraying sand everywhere.

'Fang, no! Stop it!' squeaked Max.

The puppy ignored him and carried on digging until Max grabbed him by the collar.

'You need training,' he said.

'Training?' Fang's blue eyes sparkled. 'I love trains.'

'Not trains! Training. Training is doing what you're told. So when I say sit, you sit. When I say down, you lie on the floor. And when I say fetch, you bring back the ball,' said Max.

'Sounds boring,' said Fang, lazily.

'It isn't. It's just what you need. We'll start now. It'll be fun. I promise.'

CHAPTER SIX
FULL MOON

Max spent all day with Fang. First he taught him the simple commands: sit, fetch and lie down. Then he took Fang for a walk along the beach to tire him out, in the hope that Fang wouldn't spend another night howling. It was such good fun that Max stayed out longer than he meant to. Dusk was falling when he and Fang finally arrived back at Seagull Towers. Under the cover of the trees at the bottom of the garden, Max took off his rucksack.

'In you get,' he said.

Fang shivered.

'I feel funny.'

'You are funny,' said Max. 'Hurry up and get in.'

'Look! The moon's out,' Fang stared up at the darkening sky. 'Ooh, it's huge! It must be . . .'

Suddenly Fang curled back his top lip and snarled.

'Wow! What big teeth you have,' joked Max.

'Grrrrrr!'

Fang began to tremble. 'What's happening to me?'

Tufts of longer fur were sprouting from his ears and paws. His claws grew longer and his eyes turned bluer.

'Grrrr!'

'Oh no!' groaned Max, suddenly remembering Ned's warning. 'It's a full moon. Quick! You've got to go indoors.'

'Nooooo,' howled Fang, throwing back his head and wailing loudly.

'Yes,' squeaked Max, trying to bundle Fang into his rucksack.

'Woooooo,' howled Fang, digging razor-sharp claws into the ground. 'Woooooooo!'

Bravely Max shoved Fang into his rucksack, but the werepup was turning from a fat little puppy into a lean wolf cub and fought back furiously.

'In you go,' shouted Max.

'Woooooo!' Fang yowled.

Fear gave Max extra strength. He grabbed Fang by the scruff of the neck and rammed his rucksack over the werepup's head. Fang had grown too big to fit inside, but Max held the bag in place shouting, 'Don't look at the moon!'

'Woooooo!' howled Fang, wriggling violently.

Max threw himself on the bag, pinning Fang to the ground. Fang kicked like an angry kangaroo, but Max held tight until gradually the werepup stopped struggling and fell silent. Was it his imagination or was Fang getting smaller again? Max continued to hold the puppy tightly, and after a very long while the puppy had shrunk enough to be squeezed back into the rucksack. Relieved, Max scooped the bag up in his arms and hurried towards the flats.

Max had almost reached the top of the stone steps when Fang launched a surprise attack, thrusting his head out of the top of the rucksack.

'Back!' shouted Max, struggling to push the puppy's head back in the bag.

'Wooooo!' howled Fang, gazing longingly at the moon.

Once again his top lip curled back, fur sprouted from his ears and paws, his claws grew longer and his eyes turned bright blue.

'Grrrrrrrrrrrrr,' he snarled, bursting from the rucksack just as Mrs Crab came through the revolving doors.

'A dog!' she shrieked. 'No dogs allowed. It's in the rules.'

She lunged at Fang, who darted sideways so that Mrs Crab almost fell down the stone steps.

'Sorry, Mrs Crab,' said Max politely. 'I found this puppy in the road. He's obviously a stray and I was taking him home when he escaped.'

'Get it out of here,' screeched Mrs Crab.

Fang snarled nastily and Mrs Crab turned scarlet with rage. Sticking out her enormous chest, she ran, tank-like, at him.

'Got you,' she shouted, grabbing him by the scruff of the neck. 'Ouch! Don't you try to bite me.' Mrs Crab gave Fang a hard shake as she dragged him back up the steps.

Max raced after her.

'Thanks, Mrs Crab. I'll take over now. The puppy's coming home with me.'

'I don't think so,' grunted Mrs Crab, squeezing Fang into the revolving doors. 'This is a DANGEROUS dog. First thing tomorrow I'm calling the vet to deal with it. We can't have dangerous animals running around. Now, out of my way before I have you dealt with too.'

CHAPTER SEVEN
THE ESCAPE

Max was in big trouble. There'd been a huge row at home for coming in late and his mum had sent him straight to his room after tea. Not that Max had eaten much. He was too worried about Fang. Mrs Crab had dragged Fang all the way to the boiler room, where she'd locked him inside.

Max had pleaded with her to let him take the puppy, but she'd refused and kept repeating, 'That dog is dangerous. The vet can deal with it tomorrow.'

Max hoped that Fang wouldn't feel too scared, shut up in the dark with a noisy old boiler. But Fang's comfort was the least of Max's problems. Max knew exactly what Mrs Crab had meant by getting the vet to 'deal' with Fang. She would have him put to sleep, like the dog that had chewed her favourite slippers.

'I've got to rescue Fang,' thought Max desperately.

Fang might be a bundle of mischief, but Max was already very fond of him. And what would Ned say if he knew the danger his pet was in? Miserably Max lay on his bed staring at the ceiling. Then, suddenly, he had an idea. Grinning, Max rolled over and reached for his alarm clock.

Very early the following morning Max arrived at Seagull Towers, leaned his bike against the stone staircase and tiptoed in through the revolving doors. The reception

49

hall was empty. Nervously Max glanced around before slipping behind Mrs Crab's counter. He went straight to her cabinet and rifled through the drawers. The first was jam-packed with paper clips, scissors, sticky tape and pens. The second contained a half-eaten pack of biscuits and a pile of new envelopes. But in the third Max got lucky. Right at the bottom, underneath an old newspaper, was a tin. Max opened it up and almost cheered with relief. Inside was a heap of keys, all neatly tagged and labelled.

'Boiler room,' said Max, triumphantly picking out the largest key.

He held the key tightly in his hand as he hurried across the reception hall and down the corridor to the boiler room. At first Max couldn't get the lock undone. Frustrated, he pulled the key back out and reread the label, but it was definitely the right key. Max pushed it back in slowly and jiggled it about. He was rewarded by a loud click, so he turned the handle and the door swung open.

'Woo, woo, woo,' yapped Fang, hurling himself at Max's legs as he quickly shut the door behind him. 'I'm sorry. What did I do? It must have been really bad for you to lock me up in here all night.'

Max stared at Fang in astonishment.

'Don't you remember?'

'No,' said Fang, shaking his head. 'Was I really naughty?'

'I didn't lock you up. It was Mrs Crab. You tried to bite her,' said Max.

'Nothing serious then,' said Fang, in relief.

'No, nothing serious,' replied Max.

'Except that now Mrs Crab wants to get rid of you.'

Fang wasn't listening. He had his nose inside an empty biscuit wrapper and was gobbling up the crumbs.

'I'm starving,' he said. 'I found some biscuits and guess what else I found? Come over here and I'll show you.'

'No,' said Max firmly. 'There isn't time. We've got to get out of here. This is serious. Mrs Crab is planning to have you put down.'

'Put down where?' asked Fang.

'Oh, never mind,' said Max. 'Quick, hop into my rucksack. I'm taking you out for the day so she can't find you.'

'Yippee!' squealed Fang.

He gave the biscuit wrapper one last lick, then scrambled inside Max's rucksack, but when Max turned the handle of the door it was stuck. He wiggled it and thumped it, but the door wouldn't budge. A trickle of sweat ran down Max's neck.

'Stay calm,' he told himself.

In the corner of the room Max saw a toolbox. He opened it, grabbed a hammer and gave the door handle a hard thump. There was an ominous crack, then the door swung open.

'Phew,' sighed Max, peering out into the corridor.

There was no one about. Max hared along to reception, replaced the boiler-room key, then hurried outside, almost bumping into Mrs Crab as she puffed up the stone steps.

'Good morning,' he said politely.

Mrs Crab smiled nastily.

'It will be when the vet arrives.'

'You're not ill, are you?' asked Max.

The bristles on Mrs Crab's chin wobbled furiously.

'The vet's not for me! It's for the dog that tried to savage me last night.'

'Oh,' said Max innocently. 'Of course.'

Max was keen to be as far away as possible when Mrs Crab found the boiler room empty. He unchained his bike and pedalled off as fast as he could, with Fang hidden in the rucksack, weighing heavily on his back. Max and Fang spent another great day on the beach, but this time Max was

careful not to stay out too late. He sneaked
Fang back into Seagull Towers long before
dusk. Before he went home Max drew all of
Ned's curtains so that not one chink of
moonlight could shine into the flat. Then he
made Fang promise to behave himself.

'I will,' said the puppy solemnly.

Before he left Max double-checked he'd
locked Ned's door. He was hoping to leave
unseen, but unfortunately Mrs Crab
appeared in the corridor from the boiler
room just as Max reached reception.

'You, boy!' she screeched, pointing a fat
finger at him. 'Plant sitter indeed! Well, I'm
watching you now. I know you've taken
that dog. Don't think you're going to get
away with it. I'll catch you out, and then
you'll both be for it.'

She ran her finger across her throat,

leaving Max in no doubt as to what she meant.

'And I'm watching you too,' said Max under his breath.

There was something funny about Mrs Crab. She was never around when she was needed and always there when she wasn't. Max was sure she was up to something – if only he could find out what.

CHAPTER EIGHT
FLOOD

Arriving at Seagull Towers early the next morning, Max parked his bike, then bounced up the stone staircase. He spun through the revolving doors and found an elderly lady waiting in reception.

'Good morning,' she said. 'I'm looking for Mrs Crab. Have you seen her?'

'No, sorry,' said Max.

Cheerfully he hopped up the spiral staircase. If he was quick he could smuggle Fang out of the building before Mrs Crab appeared. But as Max entered the corridor leading to Ned's flat, he could see bubbles seeping under the door. Max's heart raced. What had Fang done now? Max pulled the spider key out of his pocket, urging it to hurry as it leaped into the lock. At last the front door opened and a wall of bubbles tipped into the corridor.

'Fang!' shouted Max, pushing through them. 'Urrrg, phwwt!'

The bubbles popped around him, filling his mouth with the taste of soap. His feet squelched on the slippery carpet. Carefully Max waded along the hall and opened the kitchen door. More bubbles spilled out. Max batted them aside calling, 'Fang, where are you?'

'Here, in the sink.'

Max couldn't see as far as the sink. He paddled through the kitchen, barging into the table as he headed towards Fang's voice.

'Fang?'

'Here.'

On the draining board, looking like a bubble sculpture, sat Fang. His ears were back and he was shaking.

'What happened?' asked Max.

Fang hung his head.

'I don't know.'

'You must know.'

'I don't.'

A funny gurgling sound made Max spin round. Not far from the sink was the washing machine, and millions of bubbles were spewing from its door. Max reached over and pressed the stop button, but the bubbles continued to churn from the machine.

'I tried that already,' said Fang miserably.

'How much soap powder did you use?' asked Max. 'One lorry full, or two?'

'I didn't' squeaked Fang. 'I never touched it.'

'As if!' said Max. 'Washing machines don't just switch themselves on.'

'It did,' wailed Fang. 'I was happily chewing this stick, keeping really quiet like you told me too, when there was a green flash and the bubbles started.'

'You're always only chewing on a stick,' said Max.

'I'll chew the furniture if you'd rather,' said Fang.

'Wait!'

Max picked up the
stick and looked at it.
There wasn't much left of the
end, but he suddenly realized what it was.

'Oh, Fang!' Max couldn't help himself
and burst out laughing. 'That's not a stick.
It's a wand.'

'Yes!' Fang exclaimed. 'That's what Ned
calls it! He does really clever things with it,
even though it's only his spare.'

'What, like flooding the flat with bubbles?'

'No!' Fang's blue eyes widened. 'I
didn't . . . did I?'

Max nodded.

Suddenly Fang was laughing too. He
opened his mouth and howled.

'It's not funny,' giggled Max. He tried to
look stern, but that made him laugh even
more.

'Too right!' howled Fang. 'I nearly drowned. Can you make the bubbles go away?'

'I don't know.'

Max took some deep breaths and felt calmer. 'I could try stopping it with the wand, but it might not work now you've chewed the end.'

'Please try,' said Fang.

'Give it here then.'

'Fetch!' said Fang cheekily, throwing the wand to Max.

'Ha ha!' said Max, reaching out and catching the wand just as the kitchen door opened. He stared in horror.

'Er, hello, Mrs Crab. How did you get in?'

'The door was open,' snapped Mrs Crab. 'Why all the noise, and WHO made all this mess?'

'Me,' said Max. 'I'm doing some washing.'

'Washing?!' screeched Mrs Crab.

Her face was redder than a traffic light, and the bristles on her chin stuck out like daggers.

'NEVER, in forty years as caretaker, has anyone flooded one of my flats, until now.'

'It's Ned's flat, not yours!' growled Fang.

Mrs Crab spun round, confused. Max, finger to his lips, shook his head warningly at Fang. Fang's blue eyes widened. Then he quickly shut his mouth.

'Ha!' Luckily Mrs Crab was too angry to realize it was Fang who had spoken. 'I knew I'd catch you out in the end. It's that dangerous dog. I'm calling the vet to deal with it right now.'

Max wasn't sure what happened next. One moment he was holding Ned's wand in front of him, the next it was pointing straight at Mrs Crab's bristly chin. There was a loud crack, a strange hissing noise, then a stream of orange stars shot from the wand and whizzed around the kitchen. Max coughed. A lone star spluttered from the tip of the wand and fizzled away.

Behind him the washing machine belched loudly. Max spun round, punching the air with delight when he saw that it had finally turned itself off.

'I did it. I stopped the washing machine!' he cried, waving Ned's wand.

There was no reply. The kitchen was empty.

'Fang?' Max waded over to the sink, but Fang had gone. So had Mrs Crab, and a cold panic set in Max's stomach. Mrs Crab had taken Fang away. Something was thumping. It was louder than an army of marching giants. Max stared around the room before realizing that the noise was coming from his own heart. Suddenly he felt breathless, and that made him angry. How dare Mrs Crab take Fang away! He would follow her and demand she gave him back. As Max splashed to the door a voice called down the hall . . .

'Hello!'

CHAPTER NINE

MRS CRAB

'**I**s Mrs Crab here? I heard her voice.'

The elderly lady that had been waiting at Mrs Crab's desk in reception earlier stuck her head round the front door. Max was so relieved to see her that he laughed. For one awful moment he'd thought that Ned had come home early.

'What happened?' asked the lady kindly. 'Did the washing machine burst a pipe?'

'Several,' said Max, his brain whirring so fast he thought that it might burst too.

'Mrs Crab's gone. Didn't she pass you?'

'No, thank goodness.' The lady grinned.

'She's not the best person to meet in a narrow hallway.'

'Er, no. Quite,' said Max. 'Don't come any further. The floor's really slippery.'

Max stood in the kitchen doorway, blocking the lady's view. His heart was thumping again. He'd just noticed a large, rock-shaped creature half submerged in bubbles. It looked very out of place in Ned's kitchen. A horrible thought crossed Max's mind. No, that was ridiculous. It couldn't be, could it? Furtively Max glanced at the creature again and almost groaned out loud. This was turning into a nightmare! Max started to laugh. He always laughed when he was in trouble, even though this definitely wasn't a laughing matter.

'I need a bucket,' he said, forcing himself to be serious. 'Can you lend me one?'

'Of course I can!' said the lady. 'Back in a tick.'

Max didn't really need a bucket. He just needed the lady out of the way. When she'd gone Max shut the front door and put the chain across. Reluctantly he returned to the kitchen. The creature hadn't moved. Max bent down for a closer look at the large crab sitting on Ned's kitchen floor. It had six jointed legs, a pair of pincers, two beady black eyes and, unusually for a crab, bristles. Max prodded it with Ned's wand and the crab angrily waved a claw.

'Mrs Crab!' Max collapsed with laughter. 'Mrs Crab's turned into a crab! But how?'

'You did it.' Fang splashed through the kitchen door, and Max hugged him with relief.

'Where've you been? You gave me such a fright when you disappeared.'

'You said I was a secret so I hid.'

'Oh, Fang!' Max hugged the werepup again. 'It's too late. Mrs Crab saw you.'

'I know. So you turned her into a crab,' said Fang, chuckling.

'I didn't mean to!' Guiltily, Max stared at the wand. 'Oh bat poo!'

'But that's good! Now she can't send for the vet. Thank you, Max. You're the best pet sitter ever.'

Fang threw himself on Max, causing

a mini tidal wave that sent the crab scuttling away.

'Quick,' said Max, splashing after her. 'Shut the door before she escapes.'

Fang nosed the door shut.

'We'll have to put her somewhere safe. I know! The bath,' said Max.

He put Ned's wand on the table, but as he drew closer to Mrs Crab she snapped her enormous claws at him.

'Pinch me and I'll put you on the barbecue,' Max threatened.

Mrs Crab's shell turned scarlet. She banged a claw on the ground, splattering Max with bubbles, but she didn't pinch him when he lifted her up. She weighed a ton, and Max crossed the kitchen groaning,

'Out of the way, Fang.'

Max knew nothing about crabs, apart

from the fact that they were sea creatures. He went to the bathroom, put a few centimetres of cold water into the bath and threw in Ned's toy duck for company.

Then, shutting the bathroom door firmly behind him, he went to answer a knock at the front door.

It was the lady with two buckets and a sponge.

'Thanks,' said Max.

'Need any help?' she asked.

'No, thanks.'

'Well, if you're sure.' The lady sounded disappointed. 'If you change your mind, I'm in number sixteen.'

'Thanks,' said Max. 'And thanks for the buckets.'

When the lady had gone Max bolted the front door. Fang was sitting on the kitchen table chewing Ned's wand. Max snatched it away.

'Don't chew that!' he scolded.

'I'm a puppy. It's my job to chew things,' said Fang.

'I'm the pet sitter. It's my job to stop you,' said Max, examining the wand. The end was soggy and badly chewed. Experimentally Max waved it about. Did he dare use it to turn Mrs Crab back into herself? Perhaps he should try using it for something else first. Max decided to have a go at clearing up the kitchen.

'Stand back,' he told Fang.

Nervously Max waved the wand over a small patch of floor.

'Wand, dry. Please.'

A flash of red light burst from the wand, instantly melting the bubbles. A spiral of steam curled upwards as the floor dried.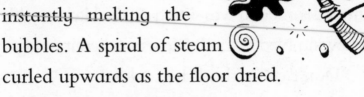

'Go, Max!' cheered Fang.

'Wicked!' exclaimed Max, and feeling braver he waved the wand around again.

'Wand, dry. Please,' he repeated.

Another flash of red. Hiss, pop, crack. The bubbles burst, sounding like a giant bowl of Rice Krispies. Steam rose from the floor and soon the kitchen was hotter than a jungle.

'Phew!' said Max, opening the window. 'That didn't take long.'

With the kitchen dry, Max started on the hall. 'Wand, dry,' he said more boldly this time.

There was a flash of red, lots of steam and a bitter smell.

'Poo!' said Max, then, realizing he'd set fire to the carpet, he waved the wand again.

'Wand, fire out.'

The flames spluttered and went out, leaving a small charred patch.

'Wicked!' sighed Fang. 'Shame about the carpet though.'

'Silly me!' agreed Max. 'Cos you'd never make a mess, would you?!'

CHAPTER TEN
FANG RUNS OFF

Max was in a dilemma. Deep down he knew he must use Ned's wand to turn Mrs Crab back into her human self. Crabby as she was (Max sniggered at the bad joke), it wasn't right to leave her in that state. But Fang was dead against the idea.

'Don't do it,' he wailed dramatically. 'She's going to have me dealt with, and what then? Ned would never forgive you.'

'But I can't leave her as she is,' said Max. 'What if she's got a family who'll miss her? We'll just have to be more careful. Especially you! No more howling and no more chewing Ned's wand.'

Before Max changed Mrs Crab back he made Fang hide in Ned's bedroom wardrobe.

'What if she comes looking for me?' he asked.

'She won't,' said Max firmly. 'I'll have Ned's wand, remember. If she tries anything funny, I'll turn her back into a crab.'

'Wicked,' said Fang. 'I hope she does.'

'Shh,' said Max as he closed the wardrobe door.

Slowly he went into the bathroom.

'Ugh!' he exclaimed. 'She must be hungry!'

Mrs Crab was eating Ned's duck; only its plastic beak remained. Experimentally Max waved the wand, then, pointing it at the bath, he said clearly, 'Wand, undo.'

There was a loud crack. Black smoke shot from the end of the wand, smothering everything. Max held his breath, wondering if his spell had worked. Then suddenly the air cleared and Max bit his tongue, trying not to laugh. There, in a bath of cold water, sat Mrs Crab. Her clothes were soaking and she had a plastic duck's beak stuck on her nose.

Max passed her one of Ned's towels, saying, 'Hello, Mrs Crab. Did you enjoy your bath?'

Mrs Crab pulled the duck beak from her nose. She shook her head a few times, then slowly stood up. Water gushed from her clothes like a waterfall.

'I'm not sure how I got here, but this I do know,' she growled. 'I'm going to catch that dog if it's the last thing I do.'

Mrs Crab climbed out of the bath and marched out of the bathroom.

Max guessed that Mrs Crab wouldn't go back to work straight away and he was right. There was no sign of her when he smuggled Fang out of the building for their daily outing. All this sneaking in and out was beginning to get to Max, and he wished there was some way of making Mrs

Crab leave him and Fang alone. After a fun day out on the beach, Max was starving and looking forward to going home for his tea. He let Fang walk to the top of Seagull Tower's drive before stopping to hide him in his rucksack.

'In you go, fatty,' he teased.

Fang stood stiller than a statue. Then suddenly he took off towards the flats.

'Fang,' shouted Max. 'Fang, come back. I was only joking.'

Fang ignored him. He raced up the stone steps and through the revolving doors. Max followed, accidentally whirling round twice before he managed to jump out. He was in time to see Fang speed off down the corridor towards the boiler room.

'Fang,' hissed Max, half cross, half scared. What was the werepup up to? He was behaving as if he wanted to get caught. When Max finally caught up with Fang he was throwing himself at the boiler-room door. Max grabbed him by the collar and hauled him backwards. Fang stuck his claws in the carpet and refused to move.

'Someone's in there,' he yapped. 'Can't you hear them shouting for help?'

Max stared at Fang suspiciously, but the werepup was serious. Then he heard it too. Inside the boiler room someone was wailing like a baby.

'I wonder who Mrs Crab's locked in there this time,' said Max angrily. 'Hello?' He banged on the door with his fist. 'Are you all right?'

There was no reply, but when Max pressed his ear to the door he heard a groan. Then he noticed the key was in the lock.

He turned it, but nothing happened. Then he wiggled the key this way and that, but the lock was jammed. He tried to force the door open. He banged and banged but it wouldn't budge.

'Shall I get Ned's wand?' offered Fang.

'No need.'

Suddenly, remembering a police raid in a film he'd watched, Max aimed a karate-style kick at the door lock. The door shuddered. Max kicked out again, and this time the lock broke and the door flew open.

'Wow!' said Fang, staring at the damage. 'How wicked was that?'

'As wicked as a hippo on ice skates,' said Max. 'But not as careful!'

CHAPTER ELEVEN
THE DEAL

Lying on the boiler-room floor, with a folding chair wedged on top of her, was Mrs Crab. She looked so funny that Max had a job not to laugh out loud. She was moaning, but she wasn't hurt and recovered

immediately when Max helped her up.

'The door lock's bust,' she grumbled. 'I couldn't get out. I was trying to unscrew the door hinges when I fell off the chair. I shouted for help but nobody came. I've been stuck in here all day.'

'That happened to me!' said Fang.

Max glared at him, wishing Fang had had the sense to hide, but it was too late. Mrs Crab spun round. Her eyes narrowed.

'It's that dog!' she exclaimed. She was too excited at having caught Max out to realize that it was Fang who'd spoken. 'And this time I'm calling for the vet.'

Mrs Crab pushed her way past Max.

'Wait,' he called. 'It was Fang who heard you shouting. He led me to you.'

'And?' said Mrs Crab nastily.

'And . . .'

Suddenly Max noticed an untidy pile of newspapers next to the boiler. He stepped closer and pulled them aside. Underneath was a kettle, a mug, a jar of coffee and several packets of biscuits.

'That's why no one can ever find you! You've been skiving off work, hiding in here drinking coffee and stuffing yourself with biscuits.'

The bristles on Mrs Crab's chin trembled and Max could see she was scared.

'You have, haven't you?' He grinned. 'Well, here's the deal: if you promise not to phone the vet and you let Fang stay here at Seagull Towers, then I won't tell anyone that you've been skiving. After all, you wouldn't want to lose your job, would you?'

For once, Mrs Crab was speechless.

★

The following day, Max and Fang sat on the steps that led up to Seagull Towers waiting for Ned to come home.

'Ooooh!' squealed Fang.

'What?' asked Max. 'Can you see Ned?'

'No.' Fang dived into the bushes. 'I need to go.'

'Again? You've only just been.'

'I can't help it,' said Fang, his black nose just visible through the branches. 'I always go when I'm excited.'

'Hurry up,' said Max. 'Ned's coming up the drive right now.'

'Oooooh!' Fang ran back and nearly knocked Max over.

'Whoa!' Max grabbed him by the collar. 'Slow down. You can't go to meet Ned like that. He'll think you're a mobile tree.'

Hurriedly Max picked leaves and twigs from Fang's coat. The werepup strained on the collar, growling like an engine. When Max finally let him go he raced towards Ned, who was staggering up the drive with two suitcases and a long package.

'Hello, hello, hello,' Fang barked. 'I've missed you soooooo much.'

'And I've missed you too,' said Ned, dumping the bags and scooping Fang up in his arms. 'Have you been good, or were you a wicked little werepup?'

'Fang's been very good,' said Max. 'We went for walks, we played on the beach and –' Max winked at Fang – 'we even did some crabbing.'

'Nothing exciting then,' said Ned cheerfully. 'Never mind, Daddy's home now and spider's teeth is he going to liven this place up! Down with silly rules! Look what my sister gave me as a thank-you for helping her out with the youth club.'

Ned pulled the paper away from the mysterious long package to reveal a shiny new skateboard.

'Wicked!' said Fang. 'Can I have a go?

'Visitors first,' said Ned, holding it out to Max.

'Thanks,' said Max, longing to try the skateboard but thinking he'd broken enough rules already, 'but I can't stop. I've got another pet to look after now. Take care, Fang! You too, Ned!'

Me and Fang!

ABOUT THE AUTHOR

Julie Sykes has had more than thirty book
published including several about her
creation, Little Tiger. Among her
other titles are *That Pesky Dragon*,
Dora's Eggs and *Hurry, Santa!*
I Don't Want to Go to Bed! and *I Don't Wan.*
to Have a Bath! won the Nottingham
Children's Book Award. Julie has three
children and lives in Hampshire.

ABOUT THE ILLUSTRATOR

Nathan Reed has illustrated children's
stories for Puffin, HarperCollins and
Campbell Books. He also illustrated one
of the most popular titles in Kingfisher's
I Am Reading series, *Hocus Pocus Hound*.
Nathan lives in London.

A selected list of titles available from Macmillan Children's Books

The prices shown below are correct at the time of going to press. However, Macmillan Publishers reserves the right to show new retail prices on covers, which may differ from those previously advertised.

Julie Sykes

The Pet Sitter: Dixie in Danger	978-0-7534-1637-2	£4.99
The Pet Sitter: Tiger Taming	978-0-7534-1636-5	£4.99
The Pet Sitter: Parrot Pandemonium	978-0-330-51046-2	£4.99

Matt Kain

Quentin Quirk's Magic Works: Attack of the Bum-Biting Sharks	978-0-330-51021-9	£4.99
Quentin Quirk's Magic Works: The Purple Sluggy Worry Warts	978-0-330-51022-6	£4.99

All Pan Macmillan titles can be ordered from our website, www.panmacmillan.com, or from your local bookshop and are also available by post from:

Bookpost, PO Box 29, Douglas, Isle of Man IM99 1BQ
Credit cards accepted. For details:
Telephone: 01624 677237
Fax: 01624 670 923
Email: bookshop@enterprise.net
www.bookpost.co.uk
Free postage and packing in the United Kingdom